P9-DDL-562

This book belongs to:

RKm 9/30/2020

Physical

Published by Scholastic Inc., 90 Old Sherman Turnpike, Danbury, CT 06816

SCHOLASTIC and associated logos are trademarks and/or registered trademarks of Scholastic Inc.

ISBN 0-7172-9874-4

Printed in the U.S.A.

Pixel's Real Test

by
Justin Spelvin

illustrated by
Artful Doodlers

SCHOLASTIC INC.

New York   Toronto   London   Auckland   Sydney
Mexico City   New Delhi   Hong Kong   Buenos Aires

Test day at LazyTown School was three days away.
Pixel asked his friends over so they could study together.
Pixel always did very well in every subject . . . except
for one.

"I'm awful at gym," Pixel told his friends. "I'm not fast. I'm not strong. Last year, I couldn't even do *one* pull-up."

"Don't worry, Pixel," Stephanie said. "We'll help you practice for the gym test, and you can help us study for math."

Robbie Rotten was listening in. He had a very rotten idea.
"I'll make that learning leader look lousy. Then all the kids
will quit the books and get back to being lazy."

A little later, a shoe salesman knocked on Pixel's door.

"You need the Speed Sneakers 3000!" he said.

"Huh?" Pixel was confused.

Pixel wanted to pass his gym test so badly that he was willing to try anything.

He laced up the sneakers and dashed outside.

With the new Speed Sneakers, Pixel could run faster and jump higher than ever before!

"Awesome!" he shouted. "If I just wear these, I'll ace that gym test!"

But when he tried to head back inside, things started to go wrong. The sneakers had a mind of their own. His feet kept moving faster and faster.

Sportacus was doing some sit-ups aboard his air ship when his crystal lit up.

"Oh no!" he said. "Looks like someone needs help!" In a flash, Sportacus was on his way.

Pixel was zooming around and around his yard. "He can't stop!" Stephanie explained.

14

"S-h-h-h-h-oes!" Pixel gasped each time he sped by.
"Maybe it's the shoes!" Sportacus guessed.

But how could they get them off Pixel's feet?

"I've got it!" said Sportacus. "Pixel, jump up and grab that tree branch. You hang on, and we'll grab the sneakers."

Pixel shook his head. If he couldn't do a pull-up, how could he hang on to the tree branch long enough to get the sneakers off?

"You can do it, Pixel," shouted
Sportacus. "Just try your best!"
"Go for it, Pixel!" the others cheered.
Pixel took a deep breath and jumped.

17

Pixel grabbed the branch and hung on with all of his might.

Trixie and Stingy pulled and pulled on the Speed Sneakers. Just as Pixel was sure he couldn't hold on any longer . . .

18

Pop! The sneakers went flying.
"You did it!" Everyone cheered.

19

Pixel was embarrassed. "I know I shouldn't have tried those sneakers on," he told his friends. "I just wanted to do well on my gym test."

"You don't need special sneakers for that," said Stephanie.

"That's right!" Sportacus agreed. "All you need to earn a good grade are the 3 P's: Practice, practice, practice!"

Pixel smiled. It was just like studying for any test.

"Let's start right now!" cheered Sportacus.

For the next two days, the gang studied and practiced.

They raced and read. They worked out their brains and their bodies.

When the big day came, everyone was prepared. They all did great on their tests.

Pixel even got a perfect score on his gym test!

"But, why didn't you wear the Speed Sneakers 3000?" asked the annoyed shoe salesman.

"Those sneakers are bad news," answered Pixel.

"They are not!" said the salesman. "Watch!"
As soon as he laced up the shoes, his feet took off.
He ran so fast, his disguise stayed behind.
"It's Robbie Rotten!" said Pixel. "Stop him!"
But Robbie was off on a long, long run.

"A little workout will do him some good," said Sportacus.

"Just like practicing did me a lot of good!" said Pixel, smiling.

Running super fast and jumping really
high felt pretty cool.
But *earning* his grade felt even better!

Nick Jr. Play-to-Learn™ Fundamentals

Skills every child needs, in stories every child will love!

 colors + shapes
Recognizing and identifying basic shapes and colors in the context of a story.

 emotions
Learning to identify and understand a wide range of emotions: happy, sad, excited, frustrated, etc.

imagination
Fostering creative thinking skills through role-play and make-believe.

math
Recognizing early math in the world around us: patterns, shapes, numbers, sequences.

 **music + movement**
Celebrating the sounds and rhythms of music and dance.

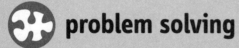 **physical**
Building coordination and confidence through physical activity and play.

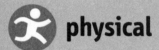 **problem solving**
Using critical thinking skills (observing, listening, following directions) to make predictions and solve problems.

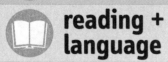 **reading + language**
Developing a lifelong love of reading through high interest stories and characters.

 **science**
Fostering curiosity and an interest in the natural world around us.

 **social skills + cultural diversity**
Developing respect for others as unique, interesting people.

Physical

Conversation Spark

Questions and activities for play-to-learn parenting.

Have a LazyTown Olympics with *your* friends! Relay races, alphabet letter dances, and counting races are great ways to work out your brain and your body just like Pixel and his friends.

For more parent and kid-friendly activities, go to www.nickjr.com.